I Went to the Bay

To Eric, my husband, and to our sons, Tony, John and Daniel — R. M.
For Sacha, my wonderful son and most astute critic — M. G.

First U.S. edition 1999

Text copyright © 1998 by Ruth Miller
Illustrations copyright © 1998 by Martine Gourbault

Kids Can Press acknowledges the financial support of the Ontario Arts Council,
the Canada Council for the Arts and the Government of Canada, through the BPIDP,
for our publishing activity. Canadä

Published in Canada by
Kids Can Press Ltd.
29 Birch Avenue
Toronto, ON M4V 1E2

Published in the U.S. by
Kids Can Press Ltd.
4500 Witmer Industrial Estates
Niagara Falls, NY 14305-1386

The artwork in this book was rendered in pencil crayon.
Text is set in Stone Sans.

Edited by Debbie Rogosin
Designed by Julia Naimska
Printed in Hong Kong by Book Art Inc., Toronto

CM   98 0 9 8 7 6 5 4 3 2 1
CM PA   00 0 9 8 7 6 5 4 3 2 1

Canadian Cataloguing in Publication Data

Miller, Ruth, [date]
    I went to the bay

ISBN 1-55074-498-4 (bound)   ISBN 1-55074-789-4 (pbk.)

I. Gourbault, Martine.   II. Title.

PS8576.I5558I29 2000   jC813'.54   C97-932811-X
PZ7.M63339Iw 1999

Kids Can Press is a Nelvana company

I Went to the Bay

written by **Ruth Miller**

illustrated by **Martine Gourbault**

Kids Can Press

I went to the bay

to look for frogs.

I saw a toad

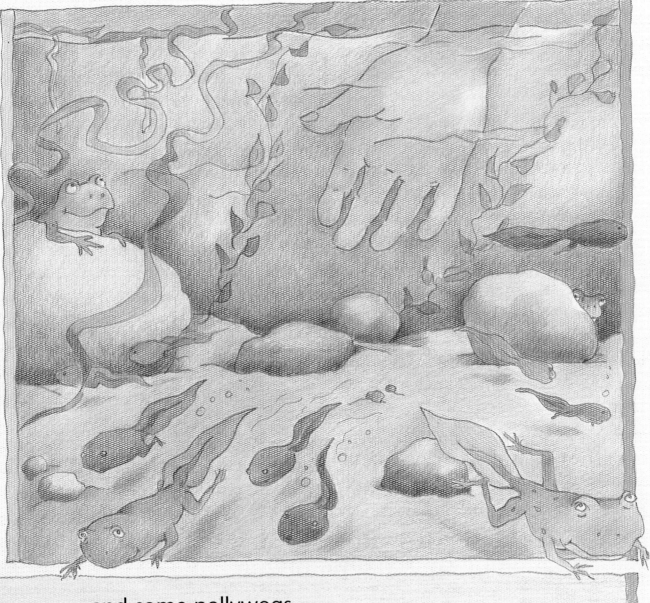

and some pollywogs.

I saw a blue heron at the edge of the bay.

This really is my lucky day!

I saw a loon and heard its cry.

A tiny hummingbird flew by.

A great big bullfrog said "harump,"

and off it went with a jump! jump! jump!

I saw a turtle come up for air,

then bury itself in the sand somewhere.

I saw a fish at the end of the dock,

and three white gulls perched on a rock.

I saw a snake go swimming by,

and a crayfish, a clam and a dragonfly.

I sat by the water under a tree.
I stayed as quiet as I could be,

and wondered if all
the creatures would say ...

I saw a human being today!

DATE DUE

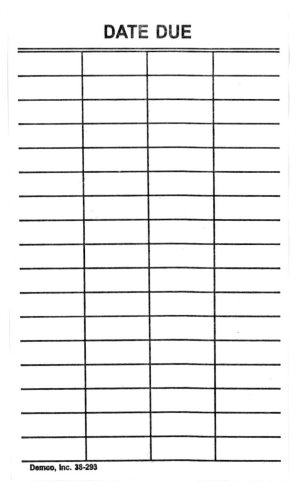

Demco, Inc. 38-293